JaBBeRWoCKy

SCARY STORIES FOR KIDS

BY
LEWIS CARROLL

AND
CAROLYN WATSON-DUBISCH

Published by Abigail Books
500 Westover Drive #10153
Sanford, North Carolina, 27330
United States of America

*"Whoever fights monsters should see to
it that in the process he does not become a monster. "
-Friedrich Nietzsche -*

So rested he by the Tumtum tree
And stood awhile in thought.

One, two! One, two!
And through and through
The vorpal blade went snicker-snack!

He left it dead,
and with its
head. He went
galumphing back.

"And hast thou slain
the Jabberwock?
Come to my arms,
my beamish boy!

O frabjous day!
Callooh! Callay!"
He chortled in his joy.

And the mome raths outgrabe.

Lewis Carroll

is the pseudonym of mathematician Charles Lutwidge Dodgson,which he adopted when publishing his famous children's novels andnonsense verse. The son of a Cheshire parson, Dodgson grewup in a large family which enjoyed composing magazines and putting on plays.

Carolyn Watson Dubisch

is a professional illustrator from New York. She's illustrated over 20 children's books, worked for Star Wars designing alien bird men and colored Wolverine and Silver Surfer comic books for Marvel. She's also written many children's books and comic books of her own.She currently lives in Mazatlán, Mexico on the Pacific coast with her husband, her youngest daughter and an unreasonable amount of pets.

Printed in Great Britain
by Amazon

23229061R00021